FOREVER MINE

IN THE DARK, BOOK THREE

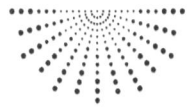

VIOLET HAZE

STOKED PUBLISHING HOUSE

Forever Mine©2016, 2019 by Violet Haze

This is a work of fiction. Names, characters, places, and incidents are the product of the author's imagination or are used fictitiously. Any resemblance to actual persons, living or dead, events, or locales is entirely coincidental.

Cover Design from Designs by Dana
Stoked Publishing House
ISBN-13: 978-0-9992261-7-9

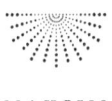

MAKSIM

I'M NOT a man who seeks perfection. However, finding a woman who fulfills my basic desires appears impossible, an opinion solidified by one failure of a date after another. This means I miss Russia.

Specifically, I miss women from Russia, many who are happy to live their lives as wives and mothers once married, raising the children and taking care of the house while the man provides financially.

Of course, I cannot return to Russia for my own safety, so I have turned to dating the women here in the USA and find many of them incompatible with my preferences.

A good example of being mismatched is the woman having dinner with me tonight.

She's sat across from me for nearly an hour now in near silence. After ordering, she sipped her water and when her salad arrived — the only item she ordered — she picked at it as if eating the whole thing would be too much for one meal.

What bothers me is that she does not appear to need to lose weight. I want a woman who takes care of herself, but this woman could do with gaining a little weight in my opinion. What man doesn't want a little something to grab onto?

However, I cannot say that to her. I have quickly learned you cannot be too blunt with many women here; they will not take kindly to hints or suggestions about what they should do. This is nothing like Russia. We wish to please each other back home, making sure to take care of our partners every need and want, while the women here are too busy making sure you know how independent they are — if you're able to get them to agree to a date in the first place.

Needing or wanting a man to take care of you is also frowned upon overall and leaves me believing I will have to find a bride from abroad anyway. Difficult when you are trying to keep the fact you are alive a secret while living under a new name for safety reasons.

The overall dating attitude is one I'm despising more with every evening spent out and when the check arrives with this one, relief doesn't begin to cover how glad I am the night is almost over. Since we drove separately, I make an excuse about needing to get up early for my flight tomorrow and by the time I arrive home, her name is already forgotten along with her number.

And I am glad tomorrow is Ramona's wedding because it means I'm getting away from the whole situation before it drives me mad in more ways than one.

SEEING RAMONA ALWAYS BRINGS A SMILE TO MY face, even after she wed another man not more than an hour ago.

If I were the type of man to keep that which isn't mine, she would still be mine, but I am not such a man. I told her the truth about everything that happened in Russia after arriving here, she chose the father of her daughter Katya, and I'm happy because she is happy.

But a woman such as Ramona is exactly what I seek in a wife, so knowing I cannot have her while also remaining lost as to where I will find another like her frustrates me and is a bit sad.

Now she dances with her new husband at their small backyard reception while I sit at this table having a drink, watching them with an unenjoyable emotion surfaces — envy.

Chandler's assistant, Joy, stares at me from where she stands near the food and drink table. Perhaps she believes her brief glances are covert, but I am not oblivious to her interest in me, especially since the day Ramona and I showed up at the house after informing Chandler we were alive.

That morning she came to meet Katya while they spoke privately, and although her red eyes made me wonder what caused her pain at that time, she had studied me with interest all while welcoming me to the country before leaving the room.

I saw her again later that evening shortly before Chandler came in to discuss his friends' arrivals the following day. After he had left the room to head to bed, she confessed her plans to have a family with Chandler and how our arrival had prevented that and continued to drink until innocent chat turned into flirting.

After putting a halt to her seduction attempts, she had burst into tears and fled from the room before I could explain my reasons. Hindsight tells me she wouldn't have been receptive to my explanation anyway, but perhaps now she will understand how I couldn't take advantage of the offer when faced with her obvious distress.

If circumstances had been different, however…

When she glances at me again, I raise my glass and smirk at her, only to frown when she turns and walks away without returning my silent greeting.

Taking that as an indication of her disinterest, there is only one thing left to do — drink and decide whether I'll be returning to the dating wasteland of America or explore other options after I head home tomorrow.

No doubt it will be the latter.

"Maksim."

Although hearing my birth name is something that rarely happens now since moving here, the name change being a necessity for protecting me, Joy being the one calling out surprises me.

The fact it's near midnight, and she's standing in the darkened hallway next to the door of the bedroom Ramona placed me in for my visit is strange and, after her reaction earlier, startling.

Stopping at the sight of her, leaving a good foot in between us, I slip my hands into my pockets and keep my tone neutral. "Is there something I may help you with, Joy?"

"I'm sorry about earlier. For ignoring you, that is." Hushed, nervous words from her that make it clear she is nervous, but about what, I am without a clue.

"No need to apologize." And that is true. We don't know each other; if she doesn't wish to speak with or have anything to do with me, that's her business. "Is that all? If so, I must say goodnight."

"You don't make this easy, do you?"

My lips curve against my will at her

exasperated huff and question. "Sorry?"

"There is something else, but can we discuss it in your room? In private?"

Her request is strange considering we're the only two people in the hall, and everyone else is in bed.

My lack of instant reply causes her to clarify while shuffling her feet. "It shouldn't take long. Please?"

Deciding this is good because it will allow me to explain my reasoning six months ago, I motion toward the door with one hand and nod even though we can barely see each other. "Ladies first."

As soon as we're inside, she shuts the door and leans against it, reaching out and placing her hand over mine to prevent me from turning on the light.

"Don't," she whispers, firming her hold on my hand and pulling it away from the wall with a soft sigh. "This will be easier in the dark."

Her statement is odd as she releases my hand, which I use to shove through my hair with a grimace. "Sorry, I don't understand. What will be easier?"

"This." She drops my hand, takes two steps and wraps her arms around my neck, pressing her lips to mine before I have the chance to process her intentions.

With all I've been through these past three years, she doesn't get an opportunity to do anything else before I've reflexively pinned her face first against the door with my body. Holding her arms above her head with one hand, I bring the other up to grab her hair in the other, wrapping it around my hand as I hiss, "Did I give you permission to touch me?"

She doesn't miss a beat, her whole body quivering with adrenaline beneath mine, matching the emotion in her words as she freezes in place. "I saw the invitation in your eyes earlier."

"You were mistaken. I only wished to speak with you and apologize for last time—"

"No." She cuts in with a gasp, pushing her ass back against my hardening cock and laughing softly when my hand tightens its grip on her hair as I groan. "Don't apologize. Just make up for it now."

"You will not tell me what to do." Tugging her head back, I decide if she's going to ask for it, she ought to know what is in store for her before we begin...just in case she wants to run like so many others do. "You're the one who takes orders, understood?"

Anticipating a gasp of shock and demand for release, her soft laugh followed by a teasing wiggle of her ass is nothing compared to the whispered phrase falling from her lips. "Yes, sir."

With any other woman who gave that answer, I wouldn't hesitate for a second to take them up on such a blatant proposition, but this is Chandler's best friend. Although we are not enemies, our neutral terms exist only because of Ramona, and since I'm under his roof…

"I can practically hear you thinking," she hisses, interrupting my thoughts while moving her ass again and moaning as my dick twitches in response to her movement. "And I know what about. I'm an adult, this is my decision to make."

Releasing her hair from my grip, I let my hand roam down her body, pleased to discover she's wearing nothing more than a thin, soft piece of lingerie that barely reaches her ass, and a flimsy thong. Joy came prepared for getting what she wants and with her warm flesh beneath my touch, there is no reason to resist giving into our mutual need.

"Keep both hands above your head, *sladkaya*, unless you wish me to end this immediately." My palms skim the sides of her body, exploring her gorgeous womanly curves before crouching behind her, stopping at the waistband of her thong to pull it down. "Step out."

Not necessary to remove the thong since I could have merely pushed the scrap covering her to the side to fuck her, but where is the fun? Rolling them in my hand while standing, I use one hand to free my cock from the restraint of my trousers and step close until she feels every inch of me against her bare ass.

Lifting the panties up to her face, I push them

against her lips, enjoying her moan and the subsequent rolling of her hips as she takes the underwear into her mouth without protest.

"Show me how quiet you can be." Gripping her hips with both hands, I lift her lower body so my cock rests between her legs and release a soft groan at how ready her body is to receive me already. "Not one sound."

She remains silent as I poise the tip of my cock at the entrance of her pussy and hold her hips still while thrusting deep inside of her. She moans and it's the most beautiful sound I've heard in a long time, especially when my pace is constant and unrelenting.

I don't reprimand her for making a noise, her walls tightening around me, letting me know she is about to come. It is a rare woman that can come from fucking alone, and her pleasure is all that is needed for me to pick up the pace, following quickly behind her.

As I release her and set her down gently, she whirls around while removing the underwear from her mouth and tosses them at me with a smile as she says, "Thanks for the quick fuck." Then she opens the door and leaves without another word, making it clear sex is the only thing she wanted.

Fine with me.

It is the perfect ending to a stressful day, and I head to bed with a genuine smile of my own for the first time in a while.

2

JOY

Six Weeks Later...

KEEPING a smile on my face as Owen and
Ramona announce that they're already expecting
another child together is hard, but I manage to
hold it together.

I moved out shortly after Ramona's return, but
I still spend a lot of time with Owen because I
work for him. Although I've continued to go out
on dates, nothing has panned out in that area, and
I've given up for now.

So, now I'm spending more time with Owen
and Ramona instead of going on dates, and that
means having dinner with them where they make
announcements like this one. It's easy to smile and
say congratulations because I am happy for him,
so that's what I do.

And although I know they are over the moon
about it, they don't gush over it, an effort I

appreciate because I know if it were me, I wouldn't be able to stop myself from displaying how thrilled having a baby made me.

Once dinner is over with, I say goodbye with the excuse of being tired and head home because I am, and cry once safely inside my place. I hate the way their announcement makes me jealous and sad simultaneously, but even more so, I hate the fact my own pain lessens the joy I would feel for them otherwise — such as when Owen found out about his daughter Katya the first time.

Ecstatic for him, honestly, even though it meant I ended our relationship and plans for a future together.

I want a child of my own, and I don't feel like I'm going to get one. Meeting a man who wants the same things I do at my age is nearly impossible, at least it seems that way since I began dating, and I'm not sure where to go from here.

Owen suggested having a child of my own, on my own, but that isn't what I want. I want a family, not just a baby. However, maybe I'm being foolish in that desire and he's right to tell me to consider single parenting as an option.

But I will think about that later. Right now I'm exhausted so hopefully after a good night's rest things will look better in the morning.

My desire for a good morning ends when I wake up nauseous with a fever and the beginning raw ache of a sore throat. After calling Owen to let him know I won't be coming to work, I take some medicine and lie on the couch, turning on the TV to keep myself occupied.

But by the evening I'm not feeling any better, even after throwing up all day while my fever spikes, and it takes the last bit of energy I have to dial my phone.

Owen answers on the second ring. "Joy, how are you feeling?"

"I think I need a ride to the hospital." The statement is scratchy, my throat burning in protest at me talking, and tears stream down my cheeks at the pain. "Please. I can barely move."

He doesn't even tell me to call 9-1-1 because he's well aware of how much I hate ambulances, only cursing beneath his breath before saying, "Be there in ten," and hanging up.

I don't even remember him showing up.

Owen's staring down at me, his hand gripping mine painfully when I wake up and discover myself in a hospital bed, fever gone and my throat hurting but not on fire like earlier.

His whole body relaxes, the worry in his face easing only for a second before he glares at me, his lips flattening in disapproval as he releases my hand and shoves one through his hair. "You scared the shit out of me. Why didn't you call for help sooner?"

"I slept most of the day other than when I was puking. I thought it would go away on its own. Been a while since I was sick like that."

He nods, leaning over to press the call button, and following that up with a kiss on my forehead before straightening. "Much better than earlier when I found you unresponsive. The doctor has only returned once since they ran some tests shortly after your arrival."

I shove away the overwhelming and unusual urge to cry at him having found me like that because I hadn't realized how seriously sick I was. "Do they know what's wrong?"

"A severe case of the flu. Not to mention extreme dehydration. You should've called sooner."

"I'm sorry. I…" My face flushes when he merely waits for me to continue and I lick my lips before lowering my gaze to admit, "After last night—"

"Joy. Look at me." His lips curve when I do, and he shakes his head before softly saying, "You are my family, and I love you. No matter what goes on in my life, you will always matter."

"I know that. I do."

Sliding his hand in his pockets, he goes back to

glaring at me. "Then knock it off. I know you as well as I do myself and don't appreciate feeling as if you've stepped back from our relationship in every single way you can after all this time."

My desire to cry grows because despite not meaning for that to happen, it has and I won't deny it. However, the doctor walks into the room right as I open my mouth to reply, and I snap it shut when he stands at the end of the bed.

He looks down at the clipboard in his hand, rambling on about how I should feel better in a few days after repeating the fact it was a severe case of the flu and after that, he looks up at me with a smile. "It's important for pregnant women to stay hydrated, Miss—"

Blinking, I cut in after a choked sound emerges from my mouth. "Excuse me? I'm not pregnant; I just had my period two weeks ago."

He looks down at his chart again and shakes his head upon returning his upbeat focus to my face. "Some women have that happen, but your hCG levels indicate you are about five weeks along."

"What?" My mind blanks, hopeful yet disbelieving and thinking he has the wrong person, and I refuse to look over at Owen right now because he won't have a hard time figuring out who the hell I slept with. "But I'm on the pill. Are you sure?"

"Yes. Congratulations, Miss James."

"Is it possible for her to have an ultrasound performed before releasing her?" Owen's question is softly spoken, and I close my eyes when he grabs my hand to give it a supportive squeeze.

After the doctor agrees and leaves the room again, Owen's eyes are filled with questions, but I refuse to answer them until I know for sure.

They keep me overnight and the next afternoon, with a pregnancy confirmation and my first ultrasound in hand, Owen drives us back to his house — asking a lot of questions on the way — to keep an eye on me until I feel better.

I don't know if that will be anytime soon because I'm pregnant with Maksim's child and have no idea what to do next.

WHEN I RETURN TO WORKING AFTER A WEEK OFF via Owen's orders, Ramona strides into his office with a big smile on her face and stops in front of the desk, her voice filled with excitement. "Is it true?"

"I'm certain Owen wouldn't have told you otherwise if it weren't."

"Oh!" She claps her hands briefly before her own smile dims, no doubt at the less than happy expression on my face, and sits down in the chair opposite me. "Is everything okay?"

"Yes. This simply isn't how I thought I would become a mother."

"I know. But, Maksim is a good man, and he will be an excellent father."

Groaning, I put my head in my hands before mumbling, "You didn't tell him already, did you?"

"Are you kidding?" She laughs and stands up as I lift my head with a skeptical smile. "I would never do such a thing because it isn't my place even if he is my friend, and if I had, he would already be here determined to take care of your every want and need."

If I didn't know so much about the man already, including her marriage to him and everything it entailed, I would think that doesn't sound so bad. But, I'm well aware of his culture and upbringing and am fairly sure I would find such a life stifling. He wants a housewife and stay-at-home mother. I've worked all my life, and yes while most of it has been for and with Owen, the thought of not working is strange to me.

"I bet. And I am thinking I would like to wait until twelve weeks. At my age...I mean my health is excellent, but just in case..."

She smiles with an understanding nod as my words trail off. "You want to wait until the chance of miscarriage is much less. Honestly, I would do the same if I were in your position, and of course, you should tell him when you're fully prepared for everything that comes with it."

"You are speaking of his propensity for being overbearing?"

"Yes, well, I never thought Owen would act that way when it comes to this pregnancy so far, but he and Maksim have much in common in that regard." She throws her hands up with a sound of exasperation and speaks with humor. "He says, 'You must eat now. Don't lift that, it's too heavy. Didn't I tell you that you should be resting?' Exhausting, especially when I did this once before and know what I am doing."

I've heard him doing these things, which is why I don't try to hide the grin or smother my laughter when Ramona blushes and lowers her hands. "And Maksim will act this way as well?"

"Worse." She clucks her tongue and whirls around, walking to the door before glancing back with a wink. "I would say I feel sorry for you, but I don't. For all the way you will want to strangle him for his ways, it is better he cares too much than too little."

Such affection in her voice for the father of my child makes my chest squeeze with jealousy, irrationally so, and even so, I trust her judgment in this.

Before finding out about the pregnancy, I hadn't thought much about that brief interlude with Maksim, other than getting a slight thrill at his treatment of me that evening.

He hadn't expected me to come onto him that

way, but he quickly turned the tables and made sure I knew he was boss, even though my encouragement had been necessary to break through his reticence about fucking me.

I briefly cursed my stupidity after realizing he hadn't used anything and got myself checked for everything within the week, but hadn't really worried because of my birth control. Still not certain how it had failed me when I took it as directed, although the doctor in the ER said my body simply may have changed and therefore caused the pill to fail.

Either way, it doesn't matter now, yet I'm still glad for the decision to wait. I may need another six weeks just to work up the nerve to break the news, as well as spend the time wondering how the hell this is going to work.

But for now, as Owen strides into the room to go over paperwork, I shove all thoughts of Maksim and the baby aside until later.

3

JOY

"You're leaving?" Owen stares at me with disbelief, his gaze bouncing back and forth between the woman and me — her name is Alicia — I've hired to help him out after my departure tomorrow. "Couldn't you have at least warned me?"

"No. I didn't want to listen to you tell me how bad of an idea this is for these past seven weeks, but now I'm out of the first trimester and need to tell Maksim."

He blinks a few times before moving his gaze back to Alicia with a dazzling smile that hides the fact he's pissed at me. "Will you please give us some privacy?"

"Absolutely, Mister Chandler," she says with a soft laugh and heads out of the room, shutting the door behind her.

That's when his smile transforms into a scowl, and he stands up, placing both his hands flat on his desk before leaning toward me with both brows raised. "What the fuck are you doing? Leaving tomorrow to fly across the country and tell him you're pregnant? Why not invite him here?"

He's worried about me, and knowing him he probably thinks I've lost my mind all of a sudden, but no matter how much we've shared everything in our lives since we met, this is one time he won't hear it all. "I think it's best I do it this way and need you to support my decision."

Mouth flattening in clear disapproval, he sits in his chair with a shake of his head and crosses his arms over his chest. "You're being ridiculous. Why go through all the trouble to train another assistant behind my back for this when you could just invite him here?"

"We both know why, Owen."

He sighs, face filling with resignation as he straightens in his seat. "Of course. You're not planning on coming back immediately. Are you sure that's the way to go?"

"Yes, but it's not me you're worried about. We both know I've got enough money to last me a lifetime, thanks to all the work we've done together. The idea of me going there, to him, that's what bothers you."

He locks his gaze with mine, searching my eyes before frowning. "This is completely out of character for you, Joy. Since when are you the type to uproot your whole life on a chance for anything or anyone?"

"The moment I made this decision because I'm going to have a child with the man is when. And Ramona assures me he will want full involvement in our child's life, so I should at least be able to see if I can handle the man on a regular basis, which means we need to spend time together before the birth. Uninterrupted."

He nods in understanding but doesn't wipe the scowl off his face. "I may disagree with the way he chose to handle things with Ramona's father and the business, but he seems like a good man, even if he chooses to live in the middle of fucking nowhere."

I love how much he cares, and his disgust amuses me enough to make me smile. "Is that it? Afraid you'll never see me except on holidays?"

"You know I'll make damn sure that never happens," he says with a laugh, finally relaxing into the chair and looking down at the desk. "Well, get Alicia in here so we can make sure we're all on the same page before you're finished tonight."

Dismissed, but I feel his eyes burning a hole into my back as I head toward the door, and my chest squeezes while the tears I'm holding back blur my vision.

Walking away from the stable place I have in Owen's life is the hardest thing I've ever done, yet

I know it's the right thing to do, even if I have no idea what tomorrow will bring.

Time to move on and my situation has given me the perfect opportunity to do so.

BY THE TIME MY FLIGHT LANDS, ALL I WANT IS A soft bed and a drink I can't have, along with a shower.

After obtaining a rental car, I pull out my phone and dial Owen's number, saying when he answers, "Hey. I made it, although my body objected to the flight in every way possible."

"Even with the medicine?"

Wincing at the concern mixed with the irritation in his voice he can't manage to hide, I say gently, "Yep. I didn't get any sleep and am exhausted, so I'll call you tomorrow after I've told him, all right?"

"You better and rest all you need. Goodnight, Joy."

"Thanks. Night."

Releasing a heavy breath of relief while hanging up, I start the car and head to the hotel where I've booked a room for the evening. I figured it would be easier to deal with everything tomorrow after some sleep rather than right after a long flight where I correctly predicted would leave me feeling like shit.

I can't wait to lie down, and when I finally get into my room, I don't even bother with a shower before climbing into the bed and dozing off.

He's not here.

Out of all the scenarios that ran through my head as I prepared to arrive here, him not even being home hadn't entered my mind.

Where in the hell could he be?

Ramona told me he doesn't have a job — he's got so much money he never has to work if he doesn't want to — nor had he mentioned being involved in anything that would take him away from home. Perhaps he went grocery shopping or something, but his grass is looking a little overgrown as if nobody has been taking care of the lawn.

Taking my phone out of my pocket, I go to dial only to see that I have zero reception, and with a sigh, I dig into my purse to pull out the set of keys Ramona gave me. She said, 'just in case' with a wink when she handed them to me and now I wonder if she knew he wasn't going to be here upon my arrival.

Heading inside, I shut and lock the door behind me before turning on a light and verifying my suspicions — nobody has been here for a while. The furniture is covered to protect it, there is a layer of dust on everything wooden, and the inside air is stale.

After opening a few windows and letting in some of the beautiful sunlight, I walk through the house while hoping to find a landline in here, and smile at the sight of a cordless phone sitting on the charger in the kitchen. Picking it up and making sure there is a dial tone, I punch in Ramona's number with a little bit of attitude and try to stay upbeat even as she answers.

"Hello?"

"Ramona, it's Joy. Listen, Maksim isn't here—"

She giggles as if this is hilarious before speaking in a hushed tone, confirming my suspicions. "Oh, I know! He apparently went out of town for a bit, but he'll be back tomorrow. I told him I've sent him a present and that it is inside the house so he's not allowed to shoot anything that moves."

If she weren't pregnant, I would've yelled at her for this, but manage to swallow my angry retort. "Oh my god, why didn't you tell me this?"

"This is more fun. He seemed happy at the thought that I've sent him something, though. Don't worry, he's not going to shoot you," she says with another laugh as the phone beeps. "Oh, I've got to go. Talk later?"

"Ramona—"

She hangs up, leaving me promising myself the next time I see her, I'm going to strangle her.

Then I decide that's irrational even if understandable, heading back outside to get the groceries I brought with me just in case, making something to eat while trying to figure out what the hell I should do now.

Apparently, it's a question I've been asking myself since discovering my pregnancy, and hope it's not going to turn into a forever thing.

I'M BAKING A PIE.

Correction, I'm baking a second pie while the first one sits on the counter cooling, all while feeling like an idiot.

Here I am, a forty-three-year-old woman, waiting on a damn man to come home, and baking like a fucking housewife. What the hell is wrong with me?

Maybe I should've given Owen the opportunity to talk me out of this ridiculous plan of mine. What did I expect? That Maksim would decide this pregnancy means we should give it a go together after I show up unannounced at his house?

Now I'm waiting for him like a damn fool, instead of going back to the hotel and trying again another day. And what in the world will he think of finding me in his house?

Swiping at the tears I can't manage to quit shedding lately sliding down my cheeks, I set the finished yet uncooked pie to the side, take off the apron, and turn off the oven before heading to the bedroom to pack the few things I took out of my suitcase.

But it's too late.

The front door opens, and Maksim's robust laughter reaches me all the way in the bedroom, quickly followed by the indistinguishable words spoken by a female who then giggles as if whatever she's said is hilarious. Her presence makes me even more upset because he's apparently seeing someone and I should have just called.

At the sound of the bathroom door closing down the hallway, I zip up my bag and lift it off the bed, only to startle at the sight of Maksim leaning against the doorjamb with a grin on his face when I turn around.

"You are leaving already?" He straightens when I frown, stepping into the room and shutting the door behind him. "Ramona sent me a message to tell me you were here; said she didn't wish for your presence to surprise me. And yet, I wonder why you are here and if you baked that pie for me."

"I made a mistake." Straightening my

shoulders, I squash the urge to look away and shrug as if it isn't a big deal or that yes, I made that pie for him. "I didn't realize you would have company, so I will go back to the hotel."

He shakes his head and widens his stance, cocking his head a little to the side with a disappointed sigh. "No. You came here for something, and now you must tell me, *sladkaya*."

"I don't." Especially not with him looking at me like he wants to rip my clothes off; thank fuck I'm not far along enough to show yet. "And I would appreciate it if you would just let me go and pretend I was never here."

"I don't like when women are ridiculous, Joy." His voice hardens, the naughty glint in his eyes dissipating as his mouth flattens in displeasure. "You will tell me why you came here to my home, now."

No chance to reply as the woman calls out, "Anton!" and opens the door without even knocking. Halting in the doorway, she stares at me as he turns around to face her.

"Leave us. I will join you in a few minutes," he answers her in Russian.

I want to smile because she obviously doesn't know I can understand what they're saying and keep my expression neutral while watching their exchange with interest.

She glares in my direction, raking her blue eyes up and down my body before tossing her blonde hair over one shoulder while scoffing, "Who is this woman? She is dirty."

"I said leave us." He grabs her elbow and glances at me while turning her toward the door. "I will return in a moment."

I do smile then and cross my arms over my chest, directing my next words —in Russian, no less — at her. "No need. If she's so curious, she can stay, especially if the relationship is serious. Becoming a stepparent in six months might change things."

Her sound of exclamation and shock followed by her mouth dropping open is amusing, but it doesn't last long as she yanks her arm from Maksim's grasp and storms out of the room while cursing loudly in Russian.

Maksim doesn't even watch her go. Instead, he focuses on me with a serious expression before chuckling and shutting the door again. Then, he walks until our bodies are inches apart and asks softly, "You are having my child? This is what you have come to tell me?"

"Yes. I am thirteen weeks along." My breath catches when he lifts a hand to my face and strokes my cheek with his thumb, not shocked by his calm demeanor thanks to Ramona's warnings yet unable to stop wondering what he's thinking. "You aren't upset I didn't call first?"

"I am too pleased with this news for anything to anger me." He leans in and presses a gentle kiss to my lips before stepping away with a nod at the bed. "You should shower and rest. I will make arrangements for Darya's return home and after we will talk, yes?"

Even while nodding, I can't resist lifting a brow and saying with exasperation, "Already bossing me around just like Ramona told me you would."

He merely laughs and shrugs. "Perhaps calling from home would have protected you from this, but now you will never know, hm?"

And with that, he leaves the room, but I don't care because I'm smiling like a fool anyway, my lips tingling from the unexpected yet completely sweet kiss that makes me sure of one thing out of all of this.

I want him to do it again when we're all alone.

4

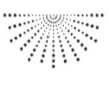

MAKSIM

DARYA IS PISSED, and I cannot blame her.

However, in an instant my life has changed, and not even how well we get along will make me change my mind.

"Your ride will be here soon." Ending the call, I set my phone down on the counter, not preventing the smile from curving my lips as she huffs again while glaring at me. "This news is unexpected. Otherwise, I never would've invited you home with me."

"How do you know the child is even yours?"

An excellent question that might stop another man from doing anything until he could get a test done, but I am not an ignorant man and know much about women's pregnancies thanks to Ramona.

And I know there is no way Joy would've said the baby is mine unless she's certain because I would bet real money on Chandler not being pleased by this turn of events.

Darya must take my silence as agreement, because she steps closer and wraps her arms around my neck, purring, "Baby, don't fall for this. It is the oldest trick in book."

Grabbing her arms, I drag them down to her sides while shaking my head at her, and step away. "You will not speak ill of my future wife and mother of my child."

She gapes at me and it is not a good look for her, nor is her expression once filled with anger. "Surely you are kidding. Even if she is having your baby, you do not have to marry her, this woman you said you hardly know yet somehow she is an American, who speaks Russian."

I am glad for the car pulling up, preventing me from having to tell her that her opinion after four months of dating isn't necessary in this matter, and lift her purse off the table. "Let me apologize for—"

"Fuck you, Anton," she hisses, snatching the purse out of my grip and storming to the front door, opening it up before looking back at me. "And I hope this bites you in the ass, you bastard."

Although the force in which she slams the door makes me wince, it doesn't wipe the smile from my face or take away how thrilled this sudden turn in my life has made me.

I am finally going to become a father and

nothing will get in my way of making sure it's done properly, bastard or no.

SEVERAL HOURS LATER, JOY STEPS INTO THE kitchen doorway, her straight black hair hanging down around her shoulders as she rubs her eyes and grumbles, "What's that smell?"

"Supper." Turning off the burner, I turn to put the food on the plates and wave a fork at the table. "Sit down so we may eat."

"No, I meant literally. That smell…"

She makes a gagging sound, covering her mouth right as I lift my head to look at her, only to grimace as she rushes over to the bin and pukes into it.

Setting the skillet down, I grab a napkin and walk over to pull her hair back from her face, rubbing her back with a sigh. "Beef stroganoff."

"Oh god," she moans, straightening after a moment and taking the napkin from my grip to wipe her mouth, her whole face flushing when her gaze finally meets mine. "Sorry. I love that, actually, just haven't had it in a long time."

"Doesn't matter, I will make you something you are able to eat."

"It isn't much." Her lower lip quivers as if she is about to cry, but she walks away before I can do anything and sits at the table. "I thought the nausea would go away by now, but it's been rough. I haven't been able to handle much beyond basic, bland foods."

"Then you will receive boring food. Tell me."

"Nothing right now, please, except a ginger ale from the fridge." After I do as she asks and take a seat across from her with my plate, she frowns at me and takes a sip from the can. "I didn't screw anything up for you, did I?"

"No. We were not at a serious point in the relationship. She will be all right."

"Okay." She takes another drink of her ginger ale before standing up and speaking softly. "Thanks for making dinner. I think I'm just going to go rest on the couch if that's all right."

Pausing my fork in mid-air, I make sure her gaze is locked with mine and smile. "Of course. This house is now yours and our child's home as much as it is mine."

Instead of nodding and breaking our eye contact to walk away, she licks her lips and lifts a hand to rub the bridge of her nose with two fingers, then sighs. "I don't understand how you're so calm about this. Don't you have any questions or concerns?"

"Yes, and we will discuss them after I finish eating. Go rest and do not worry so much. It isn't good for the child."

She purses her lips as if to say something else,

but looks away first after a few seconds and leaves me to finish dinner without another word.

TWENTY MINUTES LATER, I TURN OFF THE LIGHT after cleaning up and head into the living room, where she's lying on the couch with a pillow under her head and a blanket covering her.

"If you are cold, I will turn up the heat."

She yawns and sits up slowly, running a hand through her hair after shaking her head at me. "No, I'm fine. I sleep with something covering me even if it's hot. Just the way I prefer it."

"Ah." Instead of sitting next to her, I take a seat in the nearby chair and tilt my head backward, closing my eyes while taking a deep breath and releasing it slowly. "Your pregnancy has gone well so far?"

"Perfect, actually. I didn't find out until five weeks when I was so sick I had to go to the hospital, but everything with the baby is great."

"And you did not tell me until now?"

She sniffs, and although I am tempted to look to see if she's crying, I don't so she will focus on answering my questions rather than me watching her. "The first trimester is a higher risk for miscarriages, even more so at my age, which is why I decided to wait to say anything."

I know laughing isn't a good idea, but after a

brief chuckle, I ask, "At your age? Are you not around the same age as Chandler?"

At the sudden silence from her, I straighten in my seat and open my eyes, only to find her glaring at me. It is clear I must get used to this happening, but I shrug at her and ask, "What? You are beautiful, or we wouldn't be in this position."

It is a good thing I don't expect my compliment to do much because she looks even angrier at my statement. "And here I thought we wouldn't be in this position if my birth control hadn't failed and you had used a condom."

"Yes, it was irresponsible. Neither of us was thinking correctly in that moment, this much is clear." I wave my hand in a dismissive manner. "However, it is no longer important, so tell me what you mean by problems at your age."

She makes a 'humph' sound and crosses her arms over her chest before answering, "After age thirty-five a pregnancy is riskier. And...and after forty, the risk of miscarriage is even higher."

Genuine shock brings a smile to my face. "You are forty?"

Her blush as she answers my question is better. "Just turned forty-three."

"I had no idea. I thought you Chandler's age or younger." When she doesn't stop frowning, even in response to my compliment, I change the topic back to the pregnancy. "Either way, I remember the discussion we had that first night. I assume despite its beginning, you are excited about the pregnancy and to become a mother."

"I am." She swallows and stares down at her hands after lowering them to her lap. "It may be my only chance, so I decided even if things aren't happening as I've always wanted, it doesn't matter. That I'm having this baby."

Her vulnerability and anxiety are unmistakable, and although I want to sit next to her and comfort her, it is important to define what position I am in regards to this situation first. "I am certain you could take care of this child yourself, Joy, so tell me why you came here to me and what it is you want or need."

"Why else? I want our child to have a mother and a father who are friends and have the child's best interests at heart."

"And what kind of situation do you have in mind for this?"

"One we both agree on."

Gritting my teeth at her non-answer, I rise from my seat and watch as her gaze follows me, her eyes widening when I move to stand over her. When I crouch down between her open legs, she sucks in a breath and leans back against the cushions, slamming her eyes shut as my hands rest on her bare knees.

"There will be no agreement if the situation is one where any significant distance is between our child and me." She releases a trembling sigh as my hands skim up her legs to mid-thigh before stopping and I continue after she inclines her head to indicate she understands. "While I never desired to have a child with a woman I am not married to, it is too late for that."

She cuts in with a soft laugh even though she doesn't open her eyes. "Yes, it is, and since I am aware of your preference for a stay-at-home mother, I will say I don't believe I'm suited for such roles. I have worked my whole life."

"I am afraid I don't understand this way of thinking." My hands itch to go higher but her statement frustrates me, and I remove my touch from her, rising to my feet only to take a seat beside her. "If you are in a position where you can choose not to work and be at home with a child you say may be your only chance, why would you not take advantage of the opportunity to spend as much time with your child as possible?"

She opens one eye then and turns her head to look at me with a shrug, along with a brief biting of her lip before she says, "I don't know. Never thought about it that way. I worked for Owen for so long and loved it, but I don't need to."

"Worked? Does that mean you don't any longer?"

"Yes." A beautiful flush forms on her face as she opens both eyes but drops her gaze to her lap. "I thought...well, I hoped I could come here, and we could get to know each other while waiting for the baby to be born, and then maybe we could go from there."

Her answer pleases me because it leaves an opening for us to become more than mere co-parents, although convincing her to marry me will take some time and effort on my part, that is plain to see.

However, I am a patient man with months to get her to see things my way, so I place a hand on her knee and command her, "Look at me, Joy."

When she does with a deep, shuddering breath, it takes all my self-control to refrain from kissing her as I did earlier. Instead, I capture her free hand in mine and interlace our fingers, lifting hers to my mouth to kiss the back of it before asking, "I think that is a good plan, so I should assume you have come here with everything set already for your care?"

"Yes." Her response is a breath of a whisper, her tongue darting out to lick her lips as I hold her hand close to my mouth, until she seems to snap out of her daze suddenly and yanks free from my grip with a tight smile. "I have an appointment in a week with the new doctor and will go there more often due to my age."

"And I will attend these appointments with you."

"I didn't think you would want anything less." She lifts a hand to her mouth, yawning for a moment, and then sighs. "I believe that it's time for bed."

"You need to eat something."

"I have some crackers in the room. I will snack on a few of those and finish this, then go to sleep." She stands up, not paying me or my frown any attention, and grabs her blanket before saying, "If you want to follow me, I brought something for you."

I am not happy she isn't eating something more significant, but telling her what to do so soon will not go over so well since she is an American woman used to doing what she wishes.

When we arrive in her room, she tosses the blanket on the bed, pulls something out of her purse on the nightstand, and walks back over to where I stand near the doorway.

She holds out the paper until I take it and only says, "This is from a week ago. It's our baby."

It is one thing to talk about her being pregnant; it is another to see our child for the first time.

"Beautiful, isn't it?"

Yes, it is, but instead of saying the words, I lean in and slide my hand around the back of her neck, covering her lips with mine.

She parts them at the insistence of my tongue, moaning as she grips my shirt and steps closer until there is no space left between us.

Although it wouldn't take much for us to end

up in the same position that brought us to this moment tonight, a stable future for our child built on more than sex makes me draw back and end the kiss before it goes further.

The sight of her reddened lips and soft expression as she watches me, along with her telling me this sonogram is mine to keep, is enough to put a smile on my face.

Then, I bid her goodnight and leave her room, shutting the door behind me.

It is an excellent beginning to what I hope becomes a long-term situation.

5

JOY

"Owen, it's only been a week. Are you seriously planning to call me every day?"

"Yes." His soft laugh makes me miss him even more than I already pretend not to. "How was your appointment today?"

"Good. The new doctor seems wonderful."

"And everything else?"

"Fine."

"Just fine? Sounds like you're hovering on the line of coming back to me."

It's my turn to chuckle because, in some ways, he isn't far off on my feelings, but not so much on the coming back. "Did I say fine? I meant everything is great. Maksim is as attentive and caring as Ramona said he would be."

"I assumed as much. Otherwise, you would've been on the first flight back."

I don't know if that's true.

I won't tell him that, though. Ever since

Ramona came back into his life, the sharing of personal stuff between Owen and me has become less. Appropriately, of course, because their relationship is none of my business and the fact we had almost started a family of our own together.

However, the change has left me feeling more alone than I have our entire friendship because he has Ramona and Katya as well as a new baby on the way. He might still consider me family, and I love him for never making me feel excluded on purpose, but in some ways, he doesn't get it.

I'm smart enough to know I'm not number one priority in his life anymore, and I'm also okay with that. I shouldn't be, and that means I need to put effort into building a stable relationship with Maksim because it will be the foundation upon which we'll raise our child.

Yet, even though I rarely share my private life anymore, I want him to know how serious things could become here, so I share just a little. "Yes, it's nice he wants to be involved one-hundred-percent. He even went to the appointment earlier today. And I'm fairly positive he's interested in more since he kissed me."

I wait for a joke following a small pause of silence and Owen delivers because he never lets me down. "A kiss is pretty tame for a man who has already knocked you up. Somebody should tell him it's a bit late to take things slow."

"Funny. There is no doubt in my mind that if he could marry me tomorrow, he would."

"Ramona said something about that. Are you considering it?"

"No." When he scoffs softly in disbelief, I amend my statement because we both know the truth. "I mean, maybe? I don't know. I know what he wants and even if I've stopped working, for now, do I want to not work because I'm married to him? But he was correct also. I don't need to work, and this is my first baby, will perhaps be my only, and why shouldn't I spend every moment I can with my child?"

"I can't believe I'm going to say this, but I agree with him. I would've said the same even if you were to have a child and you were nearby, Joy. Our work together has made you a wealthy woman, and you don't need him or anybody else. No matter what your decision is about marrying him, you have the freedom to spend all your time with your child and should take advantage of it."

"I know, but working has been a big part of my life."

"I understand. You know I do because I am the same way. But you don't have to give it up completely. There are plenty of ways to fulfill your need for being productive while being a parent that don't involve working all the time."

"Like what?"

He laughs again. "If money isn't important,

volunteer. If you wish to open your own business, you could hire people to run it and directly oversee operations. You are in a unique position to do anything you want to do, Joy, and you should take advantage of having the best of both worlds, especially since you could have something set up by the time the child is born."

"You're right."

"Aren't I usually?"

That makes me smile and shake my head even if he can't see me. "No. How's Ramona?"

"Annoyed with me and my unwarranted advice, as she calls it. I love her but shit, she's moody, and I never know if what I'm going to say is the wrong thing."

Feeling sorry for him, I decide to help him out instead of leaving him in his misery to figure it out. "She doesn't mind the advice, Owen, it's how you deliver it in the form of commands or admonishments. And if you don't want her to lift something, perhaps you should do it before she chooses to do it herself. She's pregnant, not an invalid."

"I see."

I bet he does, but just in case... "Yes, well, treat her like you would treat me except much nicer because she's your wife. I'm pregnant but didn't hear you telling me not to lift a box of files at the restaurant. I'm not less pregnant than she is, and I was perfectly capable of lifting that box. Trust her, she knows what she can handle."

He sighs. "See? This is why I need you around. What will I do without you?"

"Call me just like this anytime you need a swift kick in the ass. I'll be more than happy to oblige." Yawning, I glance at the clock at the same moment my stomach growls. "I'm sure you'll call me tomorrow so we'll talk then. I'm going to make some lunch and have a nap."

"Yep, talk then."

I do exactly as I told him and am sound asleep less than forty-five minutes later.

WHERE DOES HE GO?

The next morning at nine a.m. while eating breakfast, I stare out the window to where his car is usually parked every night, but it isn't there now.

Excluding yesterday for my appointment, he leaves before I wake up and doesn't return until five or six at night. And when he gets home, he doesn't talk about his day. Since he doesn't, I don't know if he has a job or what. I know he doesn't need one, but perhaps it's something he enjoys, and I'd like to know what that is.

Every day, we make and eat dinner, he asks about my day and the baby, and then he excuses himself for the evening. Last night I asked him what he was going to do because this wasn't a way to get to know each other, and he only smiled before saying he was going to read a little then sleep.

I feel silly wanting to know what he's reading but it's more than that, too. Ever since I saw him at Owen's house that first night, I've been curious about him, and having sex with him made him more attractive.

He hasn't kissed me since that first day, however, leaving me clueless as to what will happen next with him. And knowing how he is from the night we had sex, approaching him doesn't strike me as the way to go. He might've given me exactly what I wanted that time, but now things are more delicate. I have to parent with this man carefully for the next eighteen years at the least. Screwing things up because I want a repeat of that night is the last thing I desire.

And I don't even know if he would be willing to with the pregnancy. Even dominant as I know he is, he may be one of those men who doesn't engage in anything but gentle sex when the woman is carrying a child.

Which would be better than him not wanting to have sex with me at all, but definitely not as fun.

Finishing breakfast, I stand up with a rough exhale and walk over to the sink to wash this morning's dishes, debating whether or not I want to go out and explore or if I'm already inclined to take a nap.

The nap wins out, and before I know it, I've wasted a whole day thinking about a man who probably isn't wondering about me at all.

6

MAKSIM

I WANT to touch her and not entirely in a sexual manner.

The desire to get close begins every evening when I return home and she is preparing dinner, which makes me happy because this is what I want her to do.

Although I doubt Joy has an awareness of how domestic she already is, I am positive she will be more so upon becoming a mother. Cooking, baking, and cleaning are tasks she already performs each day while I'm gone, and so far I haven't heard her speak of finding a job as I thought she would.

Due to the situation with Ramona, I know details about Joy thanks to her association with Owen, and after that night in her room, believe she will suit me perfectly now that we have this opportunity to become more familiar with each other.

Despite my behavior with Ramona under exceptional circumstances, I am not a man who will force a woman to accede to my wishes if we haven't come to an agreement about such things beforehand. I desire and aim for control; taking it is a different matter and unacceptable.

As such, while I believe we will fit well together, Joy must agree to any and all aspects of our relationship.

I have kept to myself since her arrival, giving both of us time to adjust to the change in our situations, and am confident she's taking it personally after this first week. From the moment we met in person, her every emotion flits across her face when she feels it, and nothing is hidden.

Her confusion grows and, with it, her belief I may have an interest in her beyond the child she carries.

That means I will need to give a bit more to her tonight as I suspect she will soon begin pulling away instead of trusting things to progress naturally.

All women are interesting creatures, yet something about Joy fascinates me more than any other ever has. Not able to put my finger on it right now; despite that, I am eager to move beyond this flimsy beginning to us having a relationship.

When we finish dinner, she gets up and grabs the plates to wash them as usual, while I walk into the living room to relax on the couch and watch the news. I would offer to assist, but the last time I did so, she told me she was more than capable of cleaning up after dinner. I didn't insist because she seems pleased to do it and I am sure it makes her feel useful.

Ten minutes later, she takes a seat next to me on the couch and turns to face me, frowning while crossing her arms over her chest. "What do you do all day?"

Ah, so not knowing what I am doing all day is bothering her as well. Easy enough to solve. "I am teaching at the University."

She must not have expected that answer because her eyebrows fly up, her mouth forming a short 'o' before she returns to a more neutral expression. "I see. So you do have a job, then."

"Yes, although it is more something I hope will become a permanent career."

"What are you teaching?"

"Russian, of course. Language classes for now. Am hoping they will allow me to teach a class on Russian culture beginning in the Fall semester."

She finally relaxes her body against the couch and lowers her hands to her lap. "I didn't know you were qualified to teach."

"I am from Russia, teaching Russian. What other qualifications would I need to possess?" I am kidding, of course, but she laughs even as she shakes her head and that is all that matters. All the same, I clarify my credentials. "I traded my country for helping bring down many bad people. They said they will give me anything I want to start a new life here, and this is what I used it for."

"Nice. How are the college kids treating you?"

"I believe they are pleased with being taught Russian by someone who speaks it fluently. It is most amusing to utilize it for the majority of the class as they don't understand yet."

She smirks at that. "Well, I have heard immersion is one of the best ways to learn."

"That is why my English is already much improved." She watches as I move my hand to rest on the small bump of her stomach and smiles when I say, "I will speak only Russian to our child. I may not be able to return home at this point in time, but perhaps one day, and want the child to know about the homeland."

"Of course." For a brief moment, she covers my hand with hers, and then withdraws it to drop it back at her side. "I'm sure you miss your family and your home."

"I do. My parents know I am alive as some of my men keep them informed and remain over there to protect them, although I do not fear they are in danger." She nods as I withdraw my hand from its place on her stomach and clasp mine together in my lap. "Your parents aren't alive, correct?"

She nods, frowning. "My mother died of an

aneurysm when I was thirty and my father just over a year later. Natural causes are what I was told, but I think he just…died of a broken heart."

"Were you close?"

"No, not really. I left home to work with Owen and his father. My parents wished me to stay around and weren't happy with my decision. We spoke less and less over the years after that."

"Ah."

"What about you? You brought Ramona's mother over here, why didn't you bring your parents too?"

"They didn't wish to leave. Russia is their home, and they want to remain where they were born until they die."

"I can't blame them, I guess. You get comfortable in what you know; it's hard to break free of that security for the unknown."

She speaks of herself now, of that I am sure, because her uncertainty over this whole situation is apparent.

"Do you fear the unknown, *kroshka*?"

Her cheeks flush at me calling her baby, her gaze dropping from mine once more as she nods. "My work — and indeed, my life — with Owen was predictable most of the time. No guessing, no surprises."

"And now everything has changed, but you are unsure it is for the better?"

"Well," she says after a deep breath, "I

certainly imagined becoming a mother in a less unplanned way."

"This is not the way I wanted for myself, either." Grabbing her hand with mine, I intertwine our fingers and lean forward, stopping with my face less than an inch from hers. "We will be all right, though, will we not? Both of us, we do what we must even if it isn't what we want or thought it would be."

She sucks in a breath and licks her lips, her eyes becoming hooded as she tries to hide her desire at having me close to her. "I want to believe we will be, yes." She pauses, biting on her lower lip before releasing it and asking, "Did you love Ramona?"

"Yes. We were friends for many years, and when her father told me we were to marry, I was pleased as she was everything I desired in a wife."

"You could have kept her for yourself by not telling her of Owen's visit. Why didn't you?"

I caress the tip of my thumb across her lower lip and smile. "As I said, I do what I must, even if it isn't what I want. Ramona deserved to have a life with him, the father of her child, and it wouldn't have been love to keep her when she wasn't mine."

"I wanted to keep Owen," she admits, grimacing. "I said all the right things when Ramona showed up, even when he insisted we didn't have to end things since he considered our decision a promise, but I was here when he heard the devastating news about her death. And when he realized she was pregnant with his child at the time... To have them both in front of him, alive, and to stay with me? No, I did the honorable thing while hurting so much at everything that would never be after thinking it would finally happen."

"You are human, as I am. Having those thoughts and feelings is natural. And now, those things will be, even if they aren't as you imagined — that is, you are stuck with me."

She finally laughs, her eyes opening wide when she realizes the implications. "Does that mean you're going to kiss me again?"

Sliding my hand around the back of her neck, my mouth answers her with actions instead of words, pressing against her soft lips as she inhales on a sharp breath. Her body relaxes into the couch, her arms wrapping around my neck, and her mouth opening under mine when my tongue seeks entrance.

She moans, a soft and satisfied sound as our kiss deepens, one of her arms tightening around my neck while the other spears my hair.

Dragging my mouth away, because I wish to continue this in the bedroom, her crestfallen expression amuses me as I tug her arms from around my neck and place them in her lap before standing.

Then, before any doubt sets into her mind

about my intentions, I extend my hand to her with a smile. "We will be more comfortable in the bedroom."

Seconds later, her hand is in mine, and I lead the way as she trails behind me toward a moment sure to change everything between us once again.

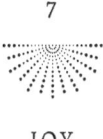

7

JOY

THERE ISN'T any doubt left in my mind about Maksim's attraction to me as he leads the way to his bedroom.

And once there, the dominant man who made clear he was the one in charge the first night we had sex reemerges, leaving me with no doubts about how this pregnancy will affect things.

That is, not much at all because I'm certain he'll do everything with care in consideration of my condition.

He shuts the door after I walk by him, then comes up behind me and places a hand on my shoulder. With the other, he moves aside my hair where it covers my neck and presses a gentle kiss on the nape of my neck.

Then he says in a commanding tone, "Take off your clothes and get on the bed."

"You're not going to help me?"

His hands leave me, one dropping to swat me on the ass. "Do as I say with no questions."

Removing my shirt as he passes on my left, I watch him stand in front of the big window across the room, staring out into the night while I'm undressing.

Will he take off his clothes, too, or is this is one way he shows he's in charge? I remember he hadn't undressed that night where he fucked me up against the door. Not that I minded.

He'd been dressed up for the wedding that day, wearing a dark blue suit and white shirt that had made me want to jump his bones. And tonight is no different, although he doesn't wear something that nice for work — he's wearing khaki-colored slacks and a buttoned up white shirt with his sleeves rolled.

Placing my clothing nicely on the chair near the wall, I walk over to the bed and lie in the center of it, waiting for him to notice I've done as requested and come over to me.

But he doesn't, not immediately, and the longer he takes, the more turned on I am. Which is no doubt his intention because the moment he pushed me against that wall and I answered him with, 'yes, sir,' he would've had me pegged me as a sexual submissive.

My legs are restless, and when I begin moving them on the bed against the soft down comforter, he says in a stern voice, "Don't move."

"Yes, sir." My answer's a bit smart as I stop shifting my legs and make my whole body remain in position without so much as a shiver.

Finally, after another few moments of silence where I'm wondering how long he's going to make me wait, I hear him move away from the window, his clothes whispering in the silence as he removes them.

He covers my naked form with his own hot one, not even using his elbows to keep his weight off me, and the way it pushes me into the bed is quite arousing, especially because I feel his cock between my legs, hard and ready to go this instant.

Not speaking, he places his lips against mine, his tongue running along the seam of mine, seeking an entrance I don't deny him. Opening my mouth, I slide my hands up and around his neck, only for him to pull away and shake his head.

"No," he says with a scowl. "Don't move."

"Yes, sir." This time, my answer is a whisper, and it's hard not to grin in response. My hands drop back to the bed, where they will remain useless and invisibly imprisoned at his command.

He goes back to invading my mouth, wanting my response but not my touch, before dragging his lips away to kiss my cheek, and then the soft skin of my neck just below my chin. His body moves in a downward direction as he presses kisses all over my chest, taking a little bit of time at each nipple

— sucking, pinching, nipping — getting them nice and pebbled before containing on his path south.

His hands keep occupied as well, skimming all over my skin — down my sides, over my middle — in direct correlation to where his mouth is, and I moan when one hand grabs my ass just as his mouth discovers the juncture between my thighs. He chuckles, his breath hot against me as he murmurs, "You smell delicious, *kroshka*."

Using his free hand, he parts my labia and within seconds, my lower body is moving into his touch while whimpers of pleasure fall from my lips as his tongue and fingers work their magic. His thumb circles my clit, avoiding direct contact, while his tongue alternates between flicking my clit or being inserted in my pussy.

He plays for what feels like forever, stopping right when my body's ready to fall over the edge, chuckling when I sob in frustration and thrust into his touch, aching for release.

Finally, when my whole body shakes in release, he doesn't even leave room for a breath between us as he glides up to cover my body once more. Using one hand, he moves my leg to wrap it around his waist while he stretches me open, easing into my body until he can go no further. Then his hand finds its way to my ass, gripping it as he begins to move.

I taste my arousal on his tongue when his mouth meets mine, his tongue wanting entrance and gaining it, thrusting in rhythm with the steady and powerful strokes of his cock. All my nerve ending sings every time he pulls to the edge before plunging in again, each inward push met by a passionate groan from him and a sound of appreciation from me.

My hands, itching to make their way into his hair, claw the comforter and clasp it in my fists to avoid breaking his rule again.

He drags his lips away enough to say, *"Tak plotnyy i vlazhnyy, kroshka."* So tight and wet.

My lips curve up at his words, and he gives an answering grin before kissing me again, increasing the pace of his thrusts until my fingers are digging into the duvet and the cry of my second orgasm is lost in his mouth seconds before he fills me with his own release on a low groan.

He remains on top of me, our mouths and tongues continuing to mingle, and after a few moments, I lift my hands and shove them into his hair.

This time, he doesn't remind me not to move, and it isn't long before we're engaging in a second session of sex, albeit a little bit gentler.

∽

A LIGHT KISS ON MY SHOULDER WAKES ME UP THE next day.

"Morning," he says against my shoulder before rolling away, the bed dipping beneath his weight.

"Morning to you." I sit up as he leaves the bed, unable to take my eyes away from his bare ass as he stands in front of the wardrobe and opens up the doors to get some clothes.

He shuts the doors and turns back to me, items in hand, and nods toward the door. "I am going to shower."

"Oh, all right." Shoving a hand through my hair, I clear my throat and toss aside the blanket, enjoying the way his gaze drops to appreciate my naked form. "I'll, um, start breakfast?"

"Yes, please." He strides back to the bed and leans over, his hand gliding into my hair to grip it before tilting my head back and capturing my lips with his for a deliciously deep kiss.

It only lasts a few seconds before he releases his hold on me and pivots, tossing the words 'twenty minutes' over his shoulder as he shuts the bathroom door behind him with a soft click.

The whole thing is so typical that, for a brief instant, I want to pinch myself to make sure it's real. Then, the tenderness between my legs as I get out of bed makes such action unnecessary, and I head to start breakfast.

By the time he enters the kitchen, there's a pile of hot pancakes on one plate and fruits — strawberries, blueberries, and sliced bananas — on another. He walks up behind me, kisses the top of my head, and grabs plates from a nearby cupboard while I pour two cups of orange juice.

When we sit down, we both fill our plates — although he goes first — and both of us proceed to eat in silence.

That's one thing I've noticed since the first day we spent together — he doesn't like to talk during meals if he can avoid it. The one night I tried to engage him, and although he humored me, I could tell he only wanted to eat and enjoy his meal without chatter, so no attempts from me since.

It will be interesting when there's a child tossed into the mix. No doubt it will be hard for him to avoid chatter during meals, especially because kids love to jabber once they've discovered language, and even before with all their noise making.

"What are you smiling about?"

I jerk my head up from where I'm staring at my plate, my brows furrowing. "What?"

He rises from his seat, his fork clinking on his empty plate, and says while turning away, "You were smiling at something. What was it?"

"Oh." I take another bite, trying to think of what to say, then decide to simply be honest as he steps up to the sink. "I was thinking about you not liking to talk during meals and wondering what you would do with a young child who talks from the moment they wake until bedtime."

He tosses a bemused smile over his shoulder and turns on the water without answering. I'm sure he's simply filling up the sink as usual for me to wash the dishes once done, but when I step up to the sink with my plate, he's soaping up to wash them.

Before I can speak, he holds out his hand for my plate and smiles at me again while taking it out of my grip. "Let me. And you go get ready."

"Ready? For what?"

"You will spend the day with me. See where I work and sit in on my classes. But we must leave soon to make it on time."

I don't miss the fact he doesn't ask me, simply tells me what I'll be doing today, and because I've wanted to know what he did all day long, turning him down to actually see him in his work would seem childish now just because he commanded instead of requested.

So I return his smile with one of my own, nod, and head out of the kitchen to get dressed for spending the day with Maksim.

8

JOY

"Did you two decide whether you want to find out the sex or not?"

I turn my head toward Maksim when the OB-GYN, Doctor Hollands, asks the question while moving the wand across my stomach.

The doctor lifts both brows in question, and I'm not sure what answer to give as we haven't even discussed whether to find out or not. Maksim's confused expression makes me laugh, and I squeeze his hand where our fingers are interlaced.

"Eighteen weeks," I clarify with a bright smile. "We can find out the sex of the baby if we want."

"Ah, I see." He clears his throat and shifts in his seat. "I didn't know that was an option."

"Yes, it is." The doctor moves the wand again, using one hand to type on the keys at the same time, and then glances back at us. "There are a few options. I will find out and tell you here, write it down and put it in an envelope if you would rather do it in private — such as at home — or if you don't want to find out, that is also fine."

I don't know if it matters to him, but I've enjoyed the wonder on his face since the moment he saw the baby moving on the screen.

I can tell he's deferring to me when he grips my hand a bit tighter and asks, "Do you wish to find out?"

Moving my gaze to the screen, I stare at it for a moment, excited in every way. "Yes, I want to know."

He nods at the doctor as she looks at him for a response before returning her focus back to the screen and shifts the wand around for a few moments. Then, she stops, lifts a hand to the screen and points to the middle of it as she says with a smile, "Congratulations, you're having a little boy."

With a tiny gasp, I place my free hand against my mouth, all while Maksim's lips slowly curve up at the news.

"A little boy," I whisper as he kisses the back of my hand, my heart fluttering with happiness.

"A son," he murmurs, clearly pleased.

When he stands up and leans over to kiss me while the doctor cleans up, this moment becomes one of the happiest in my life, and one I'll never forget.

LATER IN THE EVENING, MAKSIM AND I SIT ON THE couch after dinner. He's reading, and I'm channel surfing, which is interrupted by my phone ringing.

Picking it up from the table, I see it's Owen, so I stand up, turn off the TV, and walk into the kitchen to answer so I don't disturb Maksim.

"Hey."

"Joy," he says, a smile evident in his words. "How was the appointment?"

"Great. Found out the sex of the baby today."

"Did you?" Something shuffles on his end. "And are you going to tell me?"

"Depends." Leaning against the counter, I rub my stomach, which finally 'popped' a week ago, and sigh into the receiver. "I can't believe we haven't talked in a month."

"I know. What's kept you busy?"

"Maksim. He teaches at the University, and I've been sitting in on his classes."

He chuckles at that. "Really? I never imagined him as the teacher type."

"I honestly hadn't either, but he's terrific. His students love him. The Spring semester is over next week, and then he will do some Summer classes in July."

"Ah. I take it things are going well, then."

"Yes. Things are great. And…and I think it will be even better when our son is born."

His inhale is sharp and makes me smile. "A boy, huh? I'm thrilled for you, Joy. Hope he's just like me."

Laughing, I shake my head even though he can't see me. "Something tells me he'll be his father's son, gender roles and all."

"Nice. That reminds me...how's being a homemaker working out for you?"

"Fine. I mean, everything is so normal, you know? Reminds me of my parents in some ways. Cleaning, cooking and keeping things neat. He helps out little, but I do most of it, and there are moments where I miss working. Yet at the same time, it's nice to not have to worry about anything business related, too."

"So, are you going to start a business or no?"

"I can't say. I haven't been bored, but don't feel as if I'm fulfilling my potential on a daily basis either."

"If you ask me, the answer to the question is obvious with your response. You need to be happy, and if that means doing something more with your time outside the house and being a mother, then you should do it."

"Ugh, you're right." Sighing, I straighten away from the counter and walk over to grab a glass for something to drink. "I need something to keep me busy. I will check out the town and get back to you with some ideas. Something tells me I will need help with the decision considering this is a college town."

"Can't go wrong with food," he adds with a snicker. "Open a place with killer food and music and I doubt you'll have many problems."

Filling the glass with water, I take a sip and consider his idea for a brief moment, then say, "Well, that's definitely an idea."

"Yep. Let me know what you decide."

"I will. And now, how's Ramona doing? You being less of an unbearable ass?"

"She's great, and yes, I've gotten better about that. At least, I haven't made her as angry lately." I smile at the obvious affection in his voice for her as he continues with a light laugh. "Oh, and she says we aren't finding out boy or girl until the birth, just as she chose with Katya."

"Do you want to know?"

"Nah. It's not a big deal. A healthy baby is all that matters, she says, and I agree with her."

"Of course. Maksim was thrilled at having a boy, though. His expression said it all."

"And what about you?"

"Well, I didn't have a preference, but am happy to know."

"Good."

Maksim clears his throat behind me, and when I turn around, he's leaning against the doorjamb with a frown on his face, his arms crossed over his chest.

With a tight smile, I set my glass in the sink and tell Owen, "Hey, I've got to go for now, but I'll call you when I've got some ideas, all right?"

"Yep. Have a good night, Joy, and congratulations again."

"Thanks, you too. Night."

Pressing the red button, I slip the phone into my pocket and lift a brow at Maksim. "Is something wrong?"

"No." He straightens with a shrug, the frown on his face slipping away. "You were on the phone for a bit of time. Everything all right?"

"Yes. I was talking to Owen and catching up. We haven't spoken in a month."

"Ah, I see." He strides toward me, stopping in front of me and placing his hands on either side of my body on the sink, effectively trapping me against the counter. Smiling, he studies me for a few seconds before asking, "What are these ideas you will speak with him about?"

I lick my lips, enjoying the way his eyes drop to my mouth and bounce back nearly as quick, and take a deep breath before releasing it slowly. "Business ideas. I'm going to check out town and figure out what the city needs, what I should invest in."

His frown returns, but he doesn't move away. "You wish to work? I thought we already discussed this upon your arrival."

"We did, but I hadn't decided." At this, he

jerks away and steps back, crossing his arms over his chest once more while waiting for me to continue. "It was all new to me, Maksim, and I...I told you I've always worked. Even if I can afford not to, I want to work. It makes me happy in ways I fear being a mother never will."

"I don't understand this," he states, eyes flaring and tone flat. "You don't need to work, and a child needs a parent at home."

Annoyed, I step forward and stab him in the chest with one finger as I say, "Then why don't you stay home once the baby is born if it's that important to you?"

He clenches his jaw and glares at me before responding in a sharp voice, "That is ridiculous, Joy."

"Oh? The way I feel is ridiculous?"

"That is not what I said. I spoke of me staying home with the baby as silly as it is my duty to provide. You are our child's mother. A child needs its mother's love and nurturing." He uncrosses his arms and places a hand on each of my shoulders, his tone softening as he gazes into my eyes. "Why would you want to work when you don't need to instead of staying home and raising a family? I don't understand this way of thinking."

"Well, it doesn't matter. You are not in Russia, and I am not a Russian woman. I am an American woman who loves to work and happens to have gotten pregnant by you. And if I want to work, I will."

He drops his arms with a forceful sigh and shakes his head, his expression filling with disappointment. Then, without another word, he turns away and walks out of the kitchen.

I don't bother holding back the tears that spring to my eyes, putting my face in my hands to cry long and hard, especially knowing this is probably one thing we aren't ever going to agree on.

And later, when I head to bed, it's the first time in four weeks that we don't sleep in the same bed.

9

MAKSIM

Joy hasn't said anything besides pleasantries since our disagreement two weeks ago.

She didn't sit in on the final week of my classes at University, and although I've been home all this week due to break, she hasn't. Every morning she will make breakfast and eat, then shower and leave at nine, and not return from wherever she went until four when she prepares and cooks dinner.

Then, after washing the dishes, she'll tell me 'goodnight,' go into her room, and shut the door for the night.

I don't want to live this way, but we have a fundamental disagreement, and in this, I am hoping with some time she will bend a little. I have thought about it and still don't understand why she would want to exhaust herself by having so much to do daily.

And talking about it seems to make her angry. However, I don't enjoy sleeping apart and decide to get her back into my bed this evening, which I hope will be the first step toward working this out.

As we finish eating dinner, she stands up and grabs my plate along with hers, and walks over to wash them. I remain at the table, and when she's done, she shuts off the water before turning around, only to frown at noticing I haven't moved.

"Do you need something?"

I nod my head and stand up. "Yes, *kroshka*. I want this silence between us to end and for you to return to my bed."

She dries her hands and tosses the towel on the counter. "Unless you've changed your stance about me working, I don't see that happening."

Her stubbornness is frustrating, albeit admirable. "I wish you saw this from my point of view."

"I do understand your point of view. I just disagree with it."

"And you will not consider my feelings in this matter?"

She sighs, closing her eyes and rubbing her forehead before looking at me once more. "Maksim, I understand the culture in Russia, but it isn't the same here, and you are asking me to change everything to suit the way you want to live your life. You aren't being fair."

"You chose to come here to me." Widening my stance, I cross my arms and smile when she glares at me. "You quit working for Chandler and arrive here without warning. You step into my home and tell me we are having a child. Every day you do everything I desire you to do, act the way I want a woman I live with to act all without my request, and I am the one being unfair by asking you to do it full-time?"

"Yes!" She throws her hands up and blows out an exasperated breath. "I came here to make things easier on both of us, which I didn't have to do. I have worked my whole life and want to work now. I don't want to stay at home all day and cook and clean and wait for you to come back. I want to do something."

"You will have plenty to do when the child arrives."

"I want more in my life than motherhood and homemaking."

"I don't understand this." Shoving one hand through my hair, I place the other in my pocket and return her frown. "Why must you put so much importance on work? You want this child with all your heart, and then you will give birth, recover, and then have someone else watch the child while you work when you don't need to? Why have a child at all, then, if you will not spend a lot of time together?"

Her mouth falls open and then she snaps it shut with a sound of frustration. "How dare you say that. What about you? You will work and not spend as much time with our child. That's not any different."

"Yes, it is, and I have explained it to you."

"Oh, right," she scoffs, swiping at a tear that slipped down her cheek. "It's different because you're the man and the one who is supposed to work while I'm just expected to warm your bed, cook your meals, and have your children, correct?"

I step forward until her back is against the counter, trapping her against it, and make sure our faces are close as I give in to the temptation to make her be quiet. "Yes, that is what I would like, because having the woman who gave birth to my child — a child that may be my only — at home is what I feel will be best. You are angry with me for being exactly what you knew me to be, and now that you must face it, you fight. What are you frightened of that you will quarrel with me over this?"

Her breath hitches as she licks her lips and shakes her head. "I'm not frightened of anything."

"You are, *kroshka*. You walk into my home, please me in every way including in my bed, and choose the one thing I will not bend on to pick a fight over."

"Maybe I don't want to please you."

Impossible not to chuckle at that. I lift my hand and cup her cheek, enjoying the way she sucks in a breath and trembles beneath my touch, her eyes dilating with desire I have learned she has difficulty hiding. "Don't lie to me. There are many things I will tolerate; lying isn't among them."

"It doesn't seem like you tolerate much at all."

"I do enjoy when things are done my way, that is true."

I want to convince her the home is everything. My own mother stopped working when she married my father, and I have many fond memories of spending every day with my mother in my early years. Once I began school, she would join in on projects, volunteer, and stay engaged as much as she could, as well as continued to take care of her duties at home.

But Joy doesn't want to hear this and even though I asked, I know what she fears — that she will lose herself in the life I want for our family. There is not much I can say at this moment to make her see it isn't true because she is certain she isn't complete without working, and that is a sad way of thought.

Pressing my mouth against hers instead of saying anything more, I trace the soft fullness of her lips with my tongue, enticing her to open for me, which she does with a soft sigh in her usual fashion. The next sound from her is one of disappointment when I drag my lips away to whisper, "Let us table this discussion and spend the evening engaging in something more enjoyable for both of us."

She licks her lips and relaxes her body against mine, not fighting being in my bed as she has these past weeks. "I think that's a great idea."

"Good." Stepping back, I take one of her hands in mine and lead her toward the bedroom, shutting off the light on the way out.

When we enter the room, she sheds her clothes and places them on the nearby chair, as she's become accustomed to doing, and stares at me wide-eyed when I step in front of her as she turns to climb in bed.

I study the change in her body with a slow perusal — the noticeable increase of her bust and the swell of her stomach — and the way she stands straight with her shoulders back. The silky strands of her black hair reach the top of her shoulders, softening the angles of her face, and her intense blue eyes study me in return.

Stepping close to her, I lift my hand to her belly and run it from one side to other in a caress. "You have felt better lately?"

"Yes. The last week or so, I haven't felt sick much at all."

"Good. This means we can play tonight." Lips parting, she trembles beneath my touch as my hand slides down her stomach to between her legs, and she widens her stance with a soft gasp as my fingers touch her intimately. "Do you wish to see what it will be like between us if you let go?"

Her tongue darts out to lick her lips, her

natural submissive tendencies evident in the relaxing of her posture, and only the flashing of her eyes gives away the fact her mind battles between wanting what I can give her and anger at what she doesn't want to give me.

But finally, she surrenders to this moment with a single nod, her eyes lowering in deference to me.

Resting my hand on the top of her head, I guide her to the floor until she's on her knees, and run my hand down the length of her hair as she draws in and releases a shaky breath. "Do not worry, *sladkaya*. I will take care of you."

It is a promise made and one I intend to keep inside the bedroom, and out.

10

JOY

I DO my best not to lift my gaze from the floor when Maksim's touch leaves my hair, and at the sound of him unbuckling his belt, my entire body quivering with anticipation of what will come next.

Every inch of me craves what he will do to me. I haven't been on my knees like this since my time with Owen and even if me and Maksim are in the middle of a huge, life-changing disagreement, nothing will stop me from enjoying this evening.

"Look at me, *kroshka*." He issues the command at the same time his hand spears into my hair again, tilting my head back until our gazes collide. "Hands behind your back."

As soon as I follow his direction, he smiles and uses his free hand to guide his cock to my mouth, nudging the tip against my lips to say what he wants instead of speaking.

And there's no hesitation on my part about

opening up for him, my tongue darting out to lick him before his erection's inside my mouth. I wrap my lips around him as he passes my lips, relaxing my throat when he doesn't stop until he can't go any further, and revel in his moan along with the tightening of his grip on my hair.

He withdraws and returns, changing the pace each time so I can't be certain of when he'll shove his way back in, making sure I keep my throat relaxed to prevent gagging.

"You are beautiful." His voice is gruff as he delivers the compliment and withdraws his cock from my mouth with a tiny pop, then smiles while releasing my hair and retreating two steps. "Get on the bed. On your knees, head lowered, hands out in front of you."

When I'm in position, he secures my hands to the headboard with cuffs before moving out of my sight. His hands land on my hips, guiding my lower half until my ass is higher in the air, and the bed dips beneath his weight as he gets behind me.

Slapping one cheek playfully, he moves to the other, back and forth while increasing the speed and impact of the blows until each smack delivers an equal amount of pleasure and sting.

There's no warning before he stops and thrusts inside me, one hand gripping my hip while the other slides around my side and then in between my legs, his fingers manipulating my clit while he keeps his thrusts shallow.

His touch on my clit is too light for me to come, and combined with his dick teasing me, I want to growl in frustration. And beg for him to go faster, touch me harder, fuck me until I scream, but I know if I do, he'll just go slower because I handed control over to him.

Then, he pinches my clit and sets me off, my pussy clenching around him, and his movements become more forceful as he plunges deep.

"Oh, god." My body trembles as I moan, enjoying everything until suddenly the touch of his fingers in the cleft of my ass cause me to stiffen and stumble in my surprise. "D-don't."

He slows in fucking me again, his fingers continuing their downward path until he touches me in the one place I've never let anyone do anything and the area is sensitive enough I jump beneath his touch.

"Are you telling me no, *kroshka*?" He begins using small circular motions with a finger there — it feels like his thumb — and keeps the pressure gentle. Enough to keep me from panicking and make what he's doing seem non-threatening, so much I suddenly don't know whether I'm saying no or not and he replies to my non-response with a light chuckle. "You are inexperienced in this?"

"Yes. Anal isn't something I've desired to do, ever."

"No?"

He thrusts harder, sending frissons of pleasure

through me, and I recognize it for the distraction it is, yet it works. I forget what he's doing, merely enjoying the strokes of his cock, and being thoroughly under his command.

As he finally pushes his thumb in, my gasp is drowned out by his groan as he comes, pulsing and filling me. After, he withdraws and gently pushes my lower back until my body is flat on the bed, the front of his body resting on the back of mine. He kisses my shoulder and removes the cuffs from my wrists, rubbing them for a few seconds, then rolls off me to the edge of the bed to sit up.

I turn my head to see what he's doing, and he shoves a hand through his hair while tossing a glance my way. "I need some water. You?'

"No, thanks, I'm fine."

He nods and stands up, walking out of the room, and after a few moments, I get up to go to the bathroom. Then, once finished, I climb back into bed, slip beneath the blankets, and wait for him to return.

When he does, he settles behind me, moves one arm under my neck and places the other over my stomach, giving it a gentle caress. Kissing my shoulder, he murmurs, "Goodnight," in my ear, and it isn't long before we both drift off.

THE TOPIC OF ME STAYING HOME HASN'T COME UP

since that night four weeks ago, although it bothers him when I'm not home all day. The look he gives me in the morning when I leave is the same when I return home, and I've done my best to ignore it.

I've spent my days finding the perfect place to open up a restaurant perfect for college kids. Working with Owen made it easy to know what I need and so far, I haven't found it, but I've kept looking despite this depressing fact.

The problem is, I know Maksim will never be good with the amount of attention I'll have to give to any business venture, and so it is really a matter of time before things blow up between us once more, especially as we get closer to me giving birth.

Does it matter if he doesn't care for the way I want to do things? I say no, but I've also been alone for a long time and wonder if I'm being unreasonable and foolish.

I've juggled things for long, I'm not worried about that aspect, although I've never been a parent either, so I can't know for sure how everything will go on a daily basis.

And despite this huge issue we have, he's an amazing man. I love how passionate he is about teaching at the University; especially how happy he had been the other day when the school informed him they were going to let him teach a Russian culture course. It brings him closer to the world he had to leave behind and understand everything has much to do with how he clings to the way things are done back home.

It isn't about him denying me or wanting to control me; it all stems from thinking this is the best way to do things because that's how he was brought up.

Nothing I say will reassure him, however, and that's also a problem. I can't make him see things my way, and neither of us is going to find happiness with each other when we can't even agree on how to raise a family.

That's the whole reason I came out here. I wanted to get to know him and co-parent in peace, as friends. Hell, the first time the baby kicked, the joy in his gaze had mirrored my own, and I know we'll both be amazing parents to this child.

And yes, I had hoped we could build a relationship beyond that, but I see now that it is probably best we decide not to. It might ruin an otherwise perfect co-parenting arrangement.

Even though I've spent every night in his bed and he's slowly pushed my boundaries, showing me I can trust him repeatedly, and never taking more than I'm willing to give.

All right, the truth is, because of all this is exactly why I can't stay here. He's a good man, and I am falling in love with him — his kindness, his passion, his loyalty, and just the way he is unapologetically himself. There is no pretension, no secrets; simply a man who wants what he wants.

And he deserves more than a woman who isn't sure she can give him the one thing he wants more than anything else. Love, even if we both feel the same way, won't keep this from tearing us apart, because either he or I will be unhappy if we give in.

Maybe I am being unreasonable or foolish, and I fear nothing more than leaving him, only to regret it later. Yet, he's shown there is no compromise in this and because of it, I've made a decision.

Which leads to tonight.

As I get out of the car and shut the door — after telling my realtor I won't be buying a property after all — I head inside to tell Maksim my plans from here.

He's sitting on the couch reading when I enter and set my purse down on the table. Placing his bookmark, he stands up and puts the book back on the shelf, then turns to me with a restrained smile.

"Do not take off your shoes," he says while slipping his hands into his pockets. "We are going out to dinner."

As always, a command instead of a request, and usually I would go along with it, but tonight I shake my head. "I'm not interested in going out, I've had a long day."

"I will begin my six-week summer classes on Monday, and we will not go out much."

Sighing, I slip out of my pumps despite what he said and take a seat in the chair with a sigh, my tone exasperated. "Then you go out for dinner, and I'll find something. I'm tired."

"Of course, you are." His own voice grows tight, and I shut my eyes so I don't have to see the look on his face with what's coming next. "You are six months and running around all day."

I can't even retort how he should do more at home, then, so I don't have to after my busy day, but he already does. He probably does more than he thinks he should and if I were home all the time, he would do nothing, of that I'm certain. So, I sigh again while saying nothing and take a deep breath as he continues.

"This is why you staying home will be best. The baby will take a lot of your energy—"

"You don't know that for sure," I cut in, irritated, and open my eyes to glare at him. "Being tired and pregnant go hand-in-hand. It doesn't mean I shouldn't do what I need to do because you want what you want."

His eyes flash, his lips flattening as he stands in front of the chair and stares down at me. "Not need for you. Want."

"Maybe you should quit arguing with me

about this. I'm not changing my mind." He opens his mouth, only to snap it shut when I rise from the chair and cross my arms, our bodies not even an inch apart as I clear my throat. "Actually, we need to talk."

He must see something in my face because his expression becomes thunderous and he steps away, pushing a hand through his hair as he blows out a sharp breath.

Dropping my teary gaze, I cradle my stomach in both my hands and wonder for the hundredth time today if I'm doing the right thing. And I don't know the answer because I can't be sure of what the correct choice is, but my decision feels like the best one for me right now.

"You are going to leave?" He finally asks, his whole posture defeated as he stands before me again, but his expression doesn't give away that anything is wrong. "After all this, you will move back and have our child far away from me?"

It sounds terrible when he phrases it that way. "Yes. Plenty of people figure it out; we will, too."

"This isn't best for our child."

"Having two parents who love them is the most important thing a child needs. Not two parents who aren't happy with the way their lives are because one gave in to the other." I lift my chin when he scowls and step off to the side for a little breathing room. "I am leaving in the morning."

It's unsurprising when he doesn't ask why I'm returning to be near Owen and Ramona. They are my friends and out here, I am all alone except for Maksim. I miss them and will need their support, and he understands this without saying because he's a smart man.

Perhaps the fact he walks closer and pulls me into his warm embrace shouldn't shock me, yet it does, and words can't explain the ache in my chest when his lips take mine in a passionate, scorching kiss. His tongue shoves his, dominating and taking and searing into my memory everything I'll miss about him.

But then, he rips his mouth away, steps back and mutters, "You will regret this decision," before turning around and stalking away.

Lifting a hand to my swollen lips, my heart racing and my legs shaking, a big part of me screams how right he is. But the other part, with the stranglehold on my need for being more than a mother, yells louder.

It wins the internal argument, and the next morning, he isn't there to say goodbye, and I leave without a backward glance, a part of me wishing I hadn't bothered to come here in the first place.

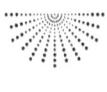

11

MAKSIM

JOY IS AN IMPOSSIBLE WOMAN.

"*Everything's fine,*" is her response to me asking her how things are going. She is nearing thirty-one weeks and yet doesn't give me many updates beyond replies such as this, no matter my efforts to speak with her.

She believes her decision the right one, and although I have disagreed from the beginning about her working, I decided after the first argument not to push it on her. I haven't been happy about it, but said nothing while holding on to the view she will change her mind once our son is born.

If not, I would have to find a way to accept it, because being away from my child would be worse than anything else.

The night before she left, I should have said it didn't matter to me, that she could work since it meant so much to her. But her decision to leave without speaking to me angered me, and I reacted in the one way guaranteed to push her in the exact direction I didn't want her to go.

I was an ass, and now she barely speaks to me.

Summer session ended on Friday, and since I have three weeks before Fall semester begins at the end of August, I am going to spend the time by visiting her. She doesn't know my plans, but Ramona does, and of course she thinks it is precisely what needs to be done.

I am surprised by how protective she is of Joy, however, and figure it has something to do with Owen's friendship with her. Ramona tells me more of what goes on than Joy does, but I know it isn't everything.

Ramona told me she wasn't happy with me, as she saw what happened as me driving Joy away with my wishes, and when her mother joined in with her opinion, it made me wonder what my own parents would think of this whole situation.

So, I informed one of my men about the circumstances the other day and asked him to relay the information to my mother — we don't communicate directly for our individual safety — and her response less than twenty-four hours later made me laugh as she said to 'quit being a stupid man.'

My mother also told me she and my father are reconsidering moving away from Russia, as they wish to have a relationship with their grandchild, and for this reason plus my own, I must make an effort to work things out with Joy.

Grabbing my bag, I make sure everything is shut off and the door is locked behind me before heading to the airport for what I hope is a trip Joy will return with me from.

RAMONA'S BEAUTIFUL AND HAPPY GRIN GREETS ME when she opens the door, rushing me inside and shutting it behind me before throwing her arms around my neck. Being as far along as Joy, her protruding stomach makes hugging her awkward, and she pulls back with a laugh when I fail at finding an appropriate position to return her embrace.

"I'm glad you're here. And you're in time for dinner." She steps away and points at my bag. "You're staying in the same room as last time if you want to put away your things first."

I glance down the hall toward the dining room and ask, "Is Joy here?"

"No," she says with a shake of her head. "She went back to her place to rest after finishing work with Owen about an hour ago."

Perfect. I came prepared to sit down at dinner with her, but now we will be alone for our first moment together since she left. Nodding, I lift my bag and return Ramona's smile. "I will take this to the room and join you in a few minutes."

"Don't take too long."

I head upstairs, drop my bag on the bed, and pull out my phone to send Joy a message. "*I would like to talk, kroshka. What time will you go to sleep tonight?*"

Usually, she will take hours to respond to my texts, but this time, she replies in seconds. "*At ten. But I don't think there is anything for us to talk about.*"

I don't want to give away the fact I will show up at her doorstep instead of speaking with her on the phone, so I slip the phone into my pocket without answering her and head down to eat.

RAMONA SENDS ME OFF TO JOY'S WITH HER address inserted into my GPS and a warning to not make Joy cry.

Perhaps I should have asked why she believes I might upset Joy, but when I finally knock on the door to Joy's apartment, and she answers, I understand why Ramona said something.

Her shocked expression is second to her red-rimmed eyes as she gasps, and even though she doesn't appear happy to see me, I am glad Ramona didn't warn her of my arrival. "What are you doing here?"

"I am here to talk." I step over the threshold

before she can shut the door in my face and lift a hand to hers, caressing her cheek with a light touch. "You have been crying, *sladkaya*."

She steps away from my touch, shuts the door, and clears her throat while leaning against it, ignoring my observation. "As I said earlier, there isn't anything to talk about, Maksim. We both know where each other stands, and it's been over a month—"

I didn't come here to argue, but it is evident she will not make this easy for either of us. I slide my hand into my pockets to avoid touching her, glancing around what appears to be her living room before smiling at her. "I had to work, and I am here now. Is that not what matters?"

"Right." She studies me for another moment, bites her lip, and then pushes away from the door with a sigh. "Okay, have a seat. Do you want something to drink?"

"Water is fine."

I take a seat on the couch as she leaves the room, returns with two glasses of water, and hands one to me before sitting in the chair to the left of me.

She sips her water, holding it with both hands, and although she waits for me to speak, I take this time to examine this beautiful woman carrying my child. Her stomach is bigger, along with her breasts; both visible in the light blue summer dress she's wearing. Combined with her hair in a bun, she looks younger, and if she were sitting next to me, I would find it difficult to keep my hands off her, so this distance is probably best.

I must have been quiet too long, however, as she sets the glass down on the table with a clink and glares at me. "You said you wished to talk, so please do before I need to sleep. Why are you here, Maksim?"

Straight to the point.

Placing my glass beside hers, I give in to the temptation to touch her and move until I'm crouched down in front of the chair and eye level with her. Then, I take her hands in mine and say, "I want you to come home with me, Joy. If you want to work, I will say nothing, and the same if you choose not to. It is up to you. You and our child are mine and belong with me."

"Do you mean it?" She whispers the question, her lower lip quivering, and at my nod, she takes a deep breath. "What made you change your mind?"

"Nothing. Like you, I want things my way, but I would rather give you what you need and raise our child together than live apart as we have been." She sniffles at that, looking unconvinced, so I tell her the one thing that might make her smile. "Plus, my mother called me a stupid man and told me I should fix it, as she wants to spend lots of time with her grandson when she and my father come to America."

Her lips lift a little at the corners, and she licks them, then her eyes round at realizing what I've said. "Your parents are going to visit?"

"They may move here. A grandchild changes things for them, and as I cannot come to Russia, they must come to me. And we must not disappoint by being unwilling to work things out even when it seems impossible." I lean in, kiss her lips, and murmur against them, "Tell me you will return home with me."

She tugs her hands from mine, shuts her eyes while inhaling then exhaling, and wraps her arms around my neck before whispering, "Yes. I would love nothing more than that because I've missed you more than I want to admit."

"You are not alone in that, *kroshka*."

"I know." She sighs and lets out a soft laugh. "There's something important I need to tell you."

"Yes?"

She opens her eyes and stares into mine as her face flushes. "I haven't worked much since coming back, although Owen tried to find me some things to do in addition to the work Alicia does, and I didn't hate the lighter load as much as I thought I would. So, earlier I was crying because I realized what a mistake I made in leaving you instead of compromising. I was trying to work up the courage to tell you that."

"And now you have." Another kiss as I smile against her lips, and she reciprocates.

"Yes, and I know you said I can work or not, so you should know that I will. I'm not sure if I'll work when the baby is little, or wait for a later time; I just know that when I'm ready, I want that option there, and I don't want you to be against it."

"Done." One of my hands finds its way around her waist, the other the nape of her neck, and my grin is mischievous as I pull back enough to gaze into her eyes. "One more thing, *kroshka*, and then we will go to bed."

"Oh, we will?" She lifts a brow, but her impish smile announces her delight at what our evening will consist of. "What is this thing delaying my rest?"

"Only that I hope you will do me the honor of becoming my wife."

There's nothing more from her than a sharp breath in before Joy, in her usual calm and collected way, answers with tears shining in her eyes. "Yes, I will."

After that, the only sounds between us are those where I demonstrate how happy her decision makes me, and she finally lets herself be mine in every way.

12

JOY

Four months later…

THERE's nothing better in the world than cradling my now six-week-old son, Nikolai, in my arms.

Well, maybe there is, especially when his father walks into the kitchen while wearing a tuxedo and steals him from my hold with a smile.

"It is time for you to get dressed, *lyubov moya.*" Maksim kisses the top of our son's head where it rests against his chest and nods toward the steps, making me feel the 'my love' he called me throughout thanks to the hot desire flashing in his eyes. "Go on. We will not be late for our wedding and keep everyone waiting."

What he means is he doesn't want to wait any longer than necessary to get me into bed since the doctor cleared me yesterday at my appointment. Only he couldn't take advantage of me last night because he had to fly in this morning after classes went on break for Thanksgiving, as we're having our wedding and reception in Owen's beautiful backyard.

Our friends and family — given and chosen, although it doesn't matter which — are in attendance, and considering the ceremony is supposed to start in less than an hour, my exaggerated sigh of reluctance is for our mutual amusement as I cross my arms over my chest and say, "Fine. I'm going."

He strides over to where I stand, pulling me against his side to kiss me without disturbing the baby, and ravishes my mouth with his until my toes curl before releasing me.

Then, he says the words I can never get enough of, that make everything better after our disagreements, and assure me our decision to work things out had been the right one.

"I love you, *kroshka*."

I cast a loving glance at our son, sound asleep on his father's chest, and then smile up into Maksim's affectionate expression. "I love you, too. See you in a bit."

"We'll be waiting," he promises before walking over to the kitchen door and heading outside, shutting the door softly behind him.

And when I'm finally ready to walk down the aisle in a simple knee-length dress that matches the blue of my eyes, Maksim waits for me at the end with a dazzling smile, our son resting in the crook of his arm.

"It isn't too late to back out," Owen teases as he steps up beside me, holding out his arm for me to take and laughs when I roll my eyes at him. "I didn't think you wanted to but had to make sure."

"I appreciate the gesture." I loop my arms through his and wait for the music to start, giving his upper arm a squeeze as I say, "And I'm so glad it's you walking me down the aisle. I wouldn't have it any other way."

"Neither would I."

We fall into silence, standing in the doorway as we are, and as I stare into my future at the end of the aisle, all that's on my mind is how much things have changed in such a short period of time.

After Maksim's proposal, we spent the rest of his vacation time with Owen, Ramona, and Katya. There were also the occasional visits from Simone and Isaac and their children — now three with their daughter, Dana, named in honor of Isaac's heritage on his father's side.

We returned home two days before the Fall semester began and spent every moment together when Maksim didn't work. This time, we were in agreement, and things were easier, especially when his parents showed up and helped prepare for the birth of their grandson.

I've put off opening my own business to ease my stress, comfortable with knowing the moment

I'm ready to dive in, Maksim will support me one-hundred percent. With that decision, I spent my time redecorating the house to turn it into more of our home, including setting up a nursery, and planned the wedding for after I gave birth.

Which I did in early October after nearly twelve hours of labor, all the pain forgotten when they laid my son on my chest, and he fed from my breast for the first time.

And as for Ramona and Owen, they welcomed their second daughter, Tatiana, three days before I had Nikolai. So he is a proud father of two and already talks about having another, which I understand because now I know the overwhelming love that comes with being a parent.

If given the chance, I can't wait to experience pregnancy all over again, especially with Maksim by my side, when we're ready for it. But now, I will enjoy having him back in my bed tonight, this time as my husband and anything that comes after will be a bonus to finally getting the life I've always wanted.

The music finally starts and at the end of the ceremony, when Maksim draws me close to his body for our first kiss as man and wife, he whispers a single word against my lips.

"Mine."

And I am, but he is also mine, and from this moment forward, nothing else matters except finding our own form of happiness and holding onto it with everything we have.

THE END!

Thanks for reading Joy and Maksim's story, the third book of the *In the Dark* series. I hope you enjoyed it! Please consider telling your friends or posting a short review on the site you purchased this book from. Word of mouth is an author's best friend and much appreciated!

www.ingramcontent.com/pod-product-compliance
Lightning Source LLC
Chambersburg PA
CBHW021025120726
47905CB00009B/3177